¡FELIZ DÍA DE LA TIERRA!/ HAPPY EARTH DAY!

By Alex Appleby

Traducción al español: Christina Green

Gareth Stevens Publishing

Please visit our website, www.garethstevens.com. For a free color catalog of all our high-quality books, call toll free 1-800-542-2595 or fax 1-877-542-2596.

Library of Congress Cataloging-in-Publication Data

Appleby, Alex.
Happy Earth Day! = ¡Feliz Día de la Tierra! / by Alex Appleby.
p. cm. — (Happy holidays! = ¡Felices fiestas!)
Parallel title: ¡Felices fiestas!
In English and Spanish.
Includes index.
ISBN 978-1-4339-9956-7(library binding)
1. Earth Day — Juvenile literature. 2. Environmentalism — Juvenile literature. 3. Environmental protection — Juvenile literature. I. Appleby, Alex. II. Title.
GE195.5 A66 2014
394.262—d23

First Edition

Published in 2014 by
Gareth Stevens Publishing
111 East 14th Street, Suite 349
New York, NY 10003

Editor: Ryan Nagelhout
Designer: Sarah Liddell
Spanish Translation: Christina Green

Photo credits: Cover, p. 1 dreamsfolklore/Shutterstock.com; p. 5 Hero Images/Lifesize/Getty Images; p. 7 Lori Adamski Peek/The Image Bank/Getty Images; p. 9 amenic181/Shutterstock.com; p. 11 Robert W. Kelley/Time & Life Pictures/Getty Images; pp. 13, 15 iStock/Thinkstock.com; pp. 17, 24 (recycle) Jupiterimages/Brand X Pictures/Getty Images; p. 19 © iStockphoto.com/Maica; pp. 21, 24 (litter) © iStockphoto.com/vgajic; p. 23 © iStockphoto.com/kali9; p. 24 (Earth) © iStockphoto.com/AntonBalazh.

Printed in the United States of America

CPSIA compliance information: Batch #CW14GS: For further information contact Gareth Stevens, New York, New York at 1-800-542-2595.

Contenido

Contents

¡El Día de la Tierra es un gran día de fiesta!

Earth Day is a great holiday!

Se celebra cada año,
el 22 de abril.

It happens every year
on April 22.

Comenzó en 1970.

It started in 1970.

Un hombre, llamado Gaylord Nelson, comenzó la celebración.

A man named Gaylord Nelson started it.

Gaylord Nelson

¡Las personas quieren ayudar a la Tierra!

People want to help Earth!

6

Quieren mantenerla segura.

They want to keep it safe.

A las personas
les gusta reciclar.

People like to recycle.

Algunas personas
plantan árboles.

Some people
plant trees.

Otras limpian
la basura.

Others clean up litter.

¡Tú también puedes ayudar a la Tierra!

You can help Earth, too!

Palabras que debes saber/ Words to Know

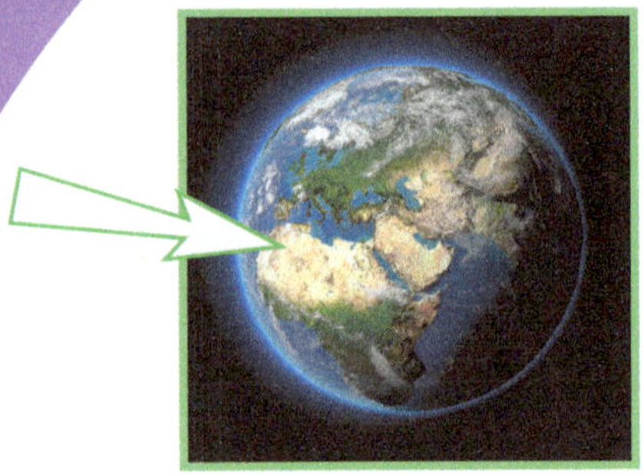

(la) Tierra/
Earth

(la) basura/
litter

reciclar/
recycle

Índice/Index